by Shannen Yauger

Cover Design by Elle Staples
Illustrated by Anastasia Khmelevska

© 2019 Jenny Phillips
goodandbeautiful.com
Printed in China

For Samantha,
who knows that a good book
will open the doorway to a
grand adventure.

Table of Contents

Anne Marie and the Reading Dog

Challenge Words

exciting

famous

librarian

poodle

Chapter One

Little Anne Marie loved to read. She read books at home and in her tree house.

She read books while Mother shopped or cleaned. Sometimes she would even read in the bathtub!

Anne Marie liked to read books about people. She liked to read books about places to visit and play.

But most of all, she liked to read books about animals—big animals, small animals, animals at the zoo, or animals in the wild. She loved them all just the same.

In her bedroom at home, she had a bookshelf of books that were just hers. Mother had her own bookshelf, as did Father.

But Anne Marie's bookshelf was meant just for her books,

and she kept them neat and in order by color—orange books, blue books, red books, and white books.

Each book color had its own place on her shelf. She called it her rainbow shelf of stories. Looking at the books on her shelf always made her very happy.

Chapter Two

One day while Anne Marie and Mother were at the library, Anne Marie saw a poster on the door.

"Come to Reading Dogs," the poster said in big bold letters. Anne Marie showed Mother the poster.

"Reading Dogs? Does that mean the dogs can read?" asked Anne Marie.

"No," said Mother as she smiled. "That means you can read to a dog. Would you like to do that?"

Anne Marie grew quiet.

Reading about animals was fun, but she was not sure she wanted to read to an animal.

Anne Marie did not have a dog and at times she was scared of them.

What if the dog stuck its nose in her face? What if the dog was very big and sat on her?

What if the dog sneezed dog

slobber on her? Or worse, what if the dog didn't like her story?

Chapter Three

Anne Marie was quiet as Mother drove home from the library. She was thinking about Reading Dogs.

Before they left the library, Anne Marie had asked the librarian about the Reading Dog.

Mrs. Apple, the librarian, was always nice and helpful when Anne Marie asked her a question.

She told Anne Marie that the dog for their library was a poodle.

Anne Marie wasn't sure what kind of dog that was.

When Anne Marie and Mother got home, Anne Marie found a book about dogs on her rainbow shelf. There, in the book under the letter "P," she found a page all about poodles.

What a big dog! She read that poodles can also be circus dogs. They are very smart, fast,

and easy to train. Anne Marie
wondered if the Reading Dog was
like this, too.

Chapter Four

At bedtime, Anne Marie told Mother that she would like to read to the Reading Dog, but she was scared of the dog.

"I understand, Anne Marie," said Mother. "What do you think you can do about your fear of the

Reading Dog?"

Anne Marie was quiet. She was thinking about what Mother had said. Mother gave her a hug then opened her bedtime book and began to read.

As Anne Marie listened to Mother read, she heard about how Daniel spent the night in a den of lions and did not fear. God was with him.

As Anne Marie said her prayers that evening, she asked God to help her with her fear of the Reading Dog.

The next morning, Anne Marie asked Mother if they could go back to the library to look for a story the Reading Dog would like.

Anne Marie found many books about dogs. She found a book about a dog that could help the blind and a book about a dog that helped at an airport. These were good stories, but not what she was looking for.

Then, she found just the right book! She quickly pulled it off the shelf and sat down to read the first three pages.

It was a story about
a poodle named Bob.
He was a happy dog
that wished for a
child to play with.
Inside the book it
showed a picture of
a little girl reading to
the poodle.

Anne Marie smiled. The girl in the story looked just like her!

Anne Marie put the other books back on the shelf where they belonged then hurried to show Mother the book she had picked out. Mother looked at the book and said, "I like this book! Would you like to check it out?"

Anne Marie nodded her head. They took it to Mrs. Apple.

She put Anne Marie on the list
to read to the Reading Dog that
week.

Chapter Five

That Friday, Anne Marie and Mother arrived at the library. Anne Marie could see the Reading Dog through the window of the reading room. She was a big dog with white fur. Her ears stood out just a little bit.

She had a fluffy head, and her bright eyes watched the young girl who was reading to her.

Anne Marie sat on a chair and kicked her feet as she waited for her turn.

The door opened, and the other girl came out, smiling.

"Anne Marie?" called Mrs. Apple.

Anne Marie took a deep breath, slid off the chair, held her book tight in her arms, and walked into the room where the dog waited.

"Anne Marie, this is Queen," said Mrs. Apple. "Would you like to pet her before you read to her?"

Anne Marie looked at Queen.

Queen looked at Anne Marie.

Anne Marie petted her head softly. Queen wagged her tail then sat down on a blanket on the floor.

"This might be okay!" thought Anne Marie. She sat down on the blanket, not too close to Queen, and began to read.

As Anne Marie read the story, Queen kept watching her with big brown eyes.

At the most exciting part of the story, Queen lifted her head and turned it sideways. Anne Marie laughed at Queen's face; it looked like she was smiling!

Anne Marie moved closer to the Reading Dog. Queen slowly put her head in Anne Marie's lap. Anne Marie smiled a happy smile and kept reading the story, all the way to the end.

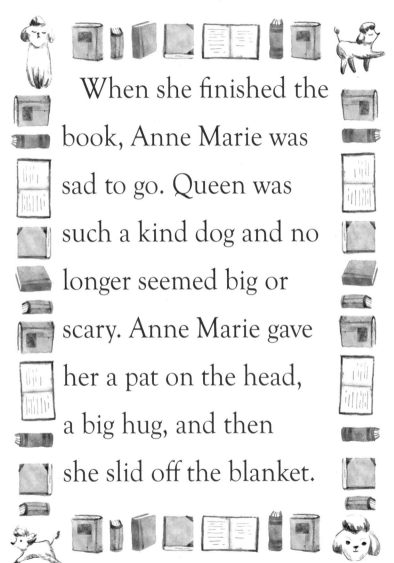

When she finished the book, Anne Marie was sad to go. Queen was such a kind dog and no longer seemed big or scary. Anne Marie gave her a pat on the head, a big hug, and then she slid off the blanket.

Queen licked Anne Marie's arm.
It was wet, but it really tickled!

With a smile Anne Marie
thanked Mrs. Apple and waved
goodbye to Queen.

Anne Marie's mother was
waiting for her outside the
Reading Dog room. Anne Marie
smiled as she took Mother's hand
and jumped up and down a bit.

"Mother," said Anne Marie,

"I would like to read to Queen again next Friday. We need to find more books with stories about dogs to share!"

When Anne Marie got home, she began to go through her rainbow shelf of stories, excited to find more books to share with Queen, her new Reading Dog friend.

The End

About the Reading Dogs Program

Wouldn't it be fun to read to a dog? Did you know that there really are Reading Dogs at many local libraries? The program may have a different name, like "Library Dogs" or "Book Pups," but the idea is still the same. You could read to a dog just like Anne Marie did in this story!

Reading Dogs are dogs called "therapy dogs," which means they are trained to not jump up or bark and to be kind and loving. These dogs stay with their handler, which is the adult that they are trained with. This adult is there to help with the dog and to listen to the story as well, but he or she may just smile and not talk much since you are there to read to the dog, not to him or her.

The Reading Dogs program is fun for every reader! It does not matter if you read fast or if you read slow. It does not matter if you are still learning and sounding out words or if you read really well. The Reading Dog is happy just to sit by you and hear you read!

Check with your local library for Reading Dog programs in your area.

Anne Marie and the Parrot

Challenge Words

bobbing

couple

parrot

tomorrow

Chapter One

Little Anne Marie loved to read. She read books at home and in her tree house.

She read books while Mother shopped or cleaned. Sometimes she would even read in the bathtub!

One sunny day, she chose a book about a small brown bear that liked to travel then she went to the front porch to read.

Just as she got to the best part of her book, she saw a car pull into the driveway of the house next door.

No one lived in that house. Anne Marie's friend, Beth, had moved four weeks ago, and the

house was empty. Anne Marie

peeked over the top of her book

to see who it was.

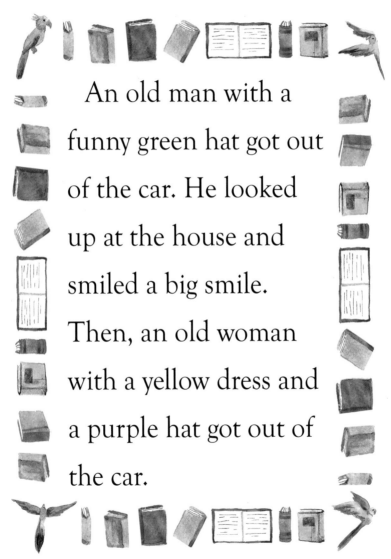

An old man with a funny green hat got out of the car. He looked up at the house and smiled a big smile. Then, an old woman with a yellow dress and a purple hat got out of the car.

She seemed very happy to be there as well. She walked over to the side of the car where the old man was waiting.

The old man with the funny green hat reached into the back seat and pulled out a large item covered with a blanket. He held it carefully as they walked up to the front door of the house and used their key to open the door.

Slowly, they went inside. Anne Marie put her book down on the

chair and ran into her house to find Mother. She could not wait to tell her about the new couple next door. They looked like they would be very nice, and Anne Marie wanted to welcome them. She also wanted to know what the old man was carrying under the blanket!

Chapter Two

"Mother!" cried Anne Marie. "A new man and a new woman went into the house next door! We have new friends!"

Anne Marie was excited to meet the new man and the new woman.

"May we make cookies for them, Mother?" Sugar cookies with red sprinkles sounded just right to welcome the new family.

Later that day when the cookies were done baking, Anne Marie and Mother walked next door with eight cookies in a bag tied with a big puffy yellow bow.

They knocked on the door. They could hear someone talking loudly. Anne Marie could hear footsteps moving very slowly. They waited.

When the door opened, the old

woman in the yellow dress smiled at Anne Marie. "Why, hello there!" she said and opened the door wide. Anne Marie smiled back. The old woman said that her name was Mrs. Smith.

"Would you like to come inside?" Mrs. Smith asked Anne Marie and Mother.

Anne Marie and Mother stepped into the house. They were greeted with a very loud "Hello! Hello! Who is there!"

Anne Marie looked around the room, smiling at the sound of the greeting.

She didn't see anyone but Mr.

and Mrs. Smith. The house was empty—no chairs, no tables, no rugs, and no books! Anne Marie looked around with her eyes open wide.

"Hello! Hello! Who is there!" She heard the greeting again.

Then, she spotted the blanket that she saw Mr. Smith bring into the house.

She looked next to it, and there

sat a parrot in a cage! Mr. Smith

saw Anne Marie stare at the

parrot.

"This is Pete," he said. "Say hello, Pete!"

"Hello, Pete! Hello, Pete! Hello! Hello!" said the parrot.

Pete had two balls hanging from ropes in his cage. He hit them over and over, which made them bump the side of the cage, and then he put his foot out to stop them.

"Hello! Hello!" he cried again.

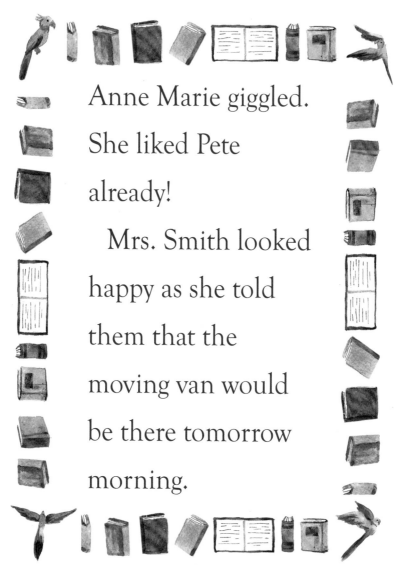

Anne Marie giggled. She liked Pete already!

Mrs. Smith looked happy as she told them that the moving van would be there tomorrow morning.

Anne Marie hoped that the moving van at least had a sofa and a bed for the Smith family!

They shared the sugar cookies with red sprinkles as a picnic on the bare floor of the living room. Mr. Smith let her give a small cracker to Pete.

"Thank you! Thank you!" Pete repeated over and over as Anne Marie laughed.

Everyone was happy. The cookies tasted even better since they were shared with new friends.

Chapter Three

The next day, Anne Marie watched as the moving van pulled into the driveway next door. Chairs, tables, lamps, pillows, and more boxes than she could count came off the van, carried by three men in grey shirts and pants. The men went back and forth from the van to the house until the last box came out. They shook hands with Mr. Smith and drove away.

Anne Marie walked next door and rang the doorbell. What a mess she saw when Mrs. Smith opened the door! Boxes piled taller than Anne Marie were stacked in every room.

"May I help you unpack?" Anne Marie asked Mrs. Smith, trying to be helpful.

"Yes, please! You can start with these boxes here," replied Mrs. Smith.

Anne Marie sat down next to a box near a bookshelf. Smiling, she started to take books out of the box.

"Oh!" she cried. "Do you like books about animals, too?"

Book after book in this box held stories of animals. Anne

Marie found books about birds, cats, dogs, frogs, horses, and even butterflies. She took a peek inside one of the books and saw such lovely pictures. Anne Marie was so happy! Look at the books just waiting to be read!

After she was done unpacking the books in that box, she looked happily at the shelf. Mrs. Smith told Anne Marie that she could

sit on the fluffy pillow next to
her and look at the books if she

would like to rest for a little bit.

Anne Marie picked out a book with a bird on the cover. The bird looked just like Pete. She sat down and began to read the book.

Mrs. Smith smiled down at Anne Marie then sat on the floor next to her. "Will you read to me now?" she asked. Anne Marie smiled at her and began to read the story.

As Anne Marie closed the book at the end of the story, she smiled. "What a lovely tale. I would like to know what it feels like to be a bird and fly up in the sky!" she said.

Just then Pete piped up.

"Fly with me! Fly with me! Hello!" he said, bobbing his head up and down.

Anne Marie laughed at him and

gave him a cracker.

He ate it and said, "Thank you! Hello!"

Chapter Four

The next day, Anne Marie woke to the sound of Pete outside her open window.

"Hello! Rise and shine! Hello!" he cried. Anne Marie hopped out of bed and peeked out of her window. She could see into the

Smith's living room.

Pete was perched on the back of a chair, his cage door open.

Anne Marie got dressed and ran to find Mother.

"Mother, may I go help Mr. and Mrs. Smith again? I'd like to see Pete, too!"

As she went across the lawn, she heard Mr. Smith say in a very loud voice, "Oh no!"

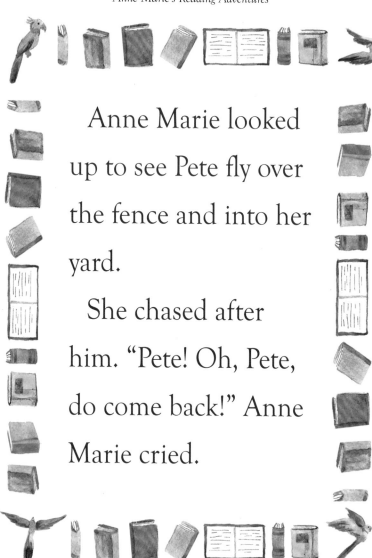

Anne Marie looked up to see Pete fly over the fence and into her yard.

She chased after him. "Pete! Oh, Pete, do come back!" Anne Marie cried.

Pete put his wings out and flew to the next tree.

"Hello!" Pete cried. "Fly away! Fly away! Rise and shine!"

"What should I do?" thought Anne Marie.

Maybe he would come to her if she had a treat to eat. That was it! Pete loved crackers! She ran into her kitchen and grabbed eight crackers.

Back in her yard, she looked for the pretty bird. She looked in each tree. He was not in her yard at all!

Anne Marie went down the street yelling, "Pete! Where are you, Pete?"

Four houses away, at a house with four flags by the front porch, she found him sitting on the porch swing.

"Here, Pete! Here is a cracker!" Pete flew under the porch flags and landed on Anne Marie's arm.

Mr. and Mrs. Smith ran to

Anne Marie. "Thank you!" they said at the same time.

"It looks like Pete wanted to have an adventure of his own!" Mr. Smith chuckled.

They all walked back to Mr. and Mrs. Smith's house with Mr. Smith holding Pete.

Anne Marie looked up at Pete and said in a stern voice, "Let's stick to *books* about flying away.

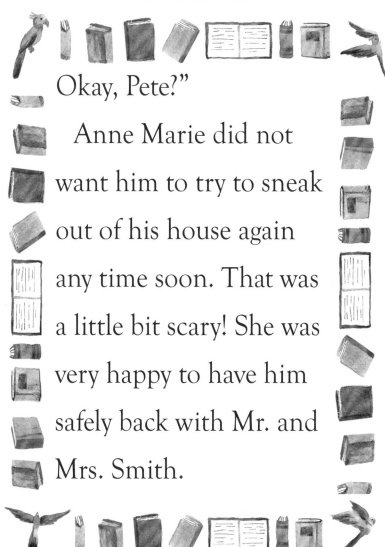

Okay, Pete?"

Anne Marie did not want him to try to sneak out of his house again any time soon. That was a little bit scary! She was very happy to have him safely back with Mr. and Mrs. Smith.

"Hello!" said Pete, spreading his colorful wings. "Fly away home!"

Everyone laughed at what Pete had said. It looked like he had learned his lesson about flying away!

The End

Anne Marie and the New Pet

Challenge Words

birthday

chocolate

counter

picture

Chapter One

Little Anne Marie loved to read. She read books at home and in her tree house.

She read books while Mother shopped or cleaned. Sometimes she would even read in the bathtub!

Anne Marie loved to read about animals, but she did not have a pet of her own. One day at lunch, while she watched snow

falling outside, Father asked
Anne Marie if she would like to
pick out a pet for her birthday.
Anne Marie was so happy!

What pet would she like to
get? The Smiths next door have
a parrot named Pete. He was fun
and silly, but he was not the pet
that she wanted. The library had
a Reading Dog. She was pretty
and fluffy, but not the pet that

Anne Marie wanted either. She went to her shelf to look at her books for help.

Anne Marie's books had a lot of animals. She pulled out one of her favorite books and turned through the pages for ideas.

The panda was cute, but Mother would not want a bear in the house. The sloth looked like it would like to cuddle, but the book said that they have a very strong smell. Anne Marie kept reading.

"A jungle tiger would not make a good pet," Anne Marie said to herself, "even if it is very pretty."

Then, she had an idea.

"Father!" she cried, as she ran to the kitchen. "Father, may I get a tiger kitten?"

She showed Father a picture of a small striped kitten in her book. The kitten was orange with little brown stripes and a big red bow around his neck. Father smiled and nodded. A striped kitten sounded like a perfect pet for Anne Marie.

Anne Marie carried the book back to her room and set it on her desk. She could not wait for it to be her birthday. Father had said she could have a striped kitten!

Chapter Two

On the morning of her birthday, Anne Marie could not sleep. She jumped out of bed and ran downstairs to the kitchen. Mother and Father were already awake and were making pancakes. On the table was a big box with a blue bow on top.

As she looked closer, Anne Marie saw the box wiggle just a little bit.

"Oh!" she cried. "May I open the box, please?"

Anne Marie carefully took the lid off the box. Inside sat the cutest tiger kitten she had ever seen! He looked just like the picture of the little kitten she had seen in her book.

"Meow!" said the little kitten, swatting at his blue bow. He was so small and sweet!

She lifted her new pet out of the box and set him in her lap.

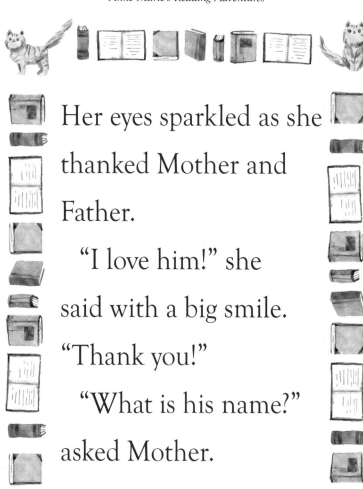

Her eyes sparkled as she thanked Mother and Father.

"I love him!" she said with a big smile. "Thank you!"

"What is his name?" asked Mother.

"I am not sure yet," said Anne Marie. "I need to get to know him first."

After she ate breakfast, Anne Marie went to her room to let the kitten play. She set him down on the floor. Slowly her little kitten began to look around her room.

"Jack?" thought Anne Marie, looking at the kitten. "No, that's not right."

When he grew tired of exploring her closet, he jumped onto her bed and fell asleep.

"Tiger? No, he won't be that big." Anne Marie could not think of a name for her cute kitten.

Chapter Three

As the kitten napped, Anne Marie looked at the books on her shelf. Maybe she could find a book that would help her name the kitten. She looked at all of her books about cats. She found a story about a shy little kitten and one about big cats in the wild. She found one about a cat that got stuck in a tree and one that took a ride in a car.

None of the stories had a good name for her new kitten. Anne Marie needed to see how her kitten acted before she could name him. His name needed to fit *him*, not a cat in her books.

Anne Marie kept thinking.

When her kitten woke
up from a short nap,
Anne Marie took him
back to the kitchen
where Mother was
baking cookies. One
plate of cookies sat on
the counter.

Mother was mixing a fresh batch of cookies in a large red bowl.

As she added the chocolate chips to the batter, the little kitten jumped out of Anne Marie's arms and onto the table, spilling some of the chips out of Mother's box!

The chocolate chips spilled all over the counter and onto the floor. Some of them even fell into the sink that was full of dishes from baking. Even more rolled onto the floor, and the kitten jumped toward them.

"Oh no!" cried Anne Marie as she ran to grab her kitten. "Do not eat the chocolate, little kitten!"

"Meow!" responded her little pet. He looked at her and swished his tail. Anne Marie helped Mother clean up then took her kitten to the playroom.

As soon as she set him on the floor, he ran for her blocks that she'd made into a tower.

"Look out!" cried Anne Marie. The kitten slid into the tall tower of blocks, and the tower fell with a loud crash to the floor. The kitten pounced on the pile of blocks. Anne Marie laughed at him and gave him a hug.

Chapter Four

Anne Marie and her kitten went to the living room, as it was safer with fewer things to break or spill. She picked a book from her bookshelf and sat down on a fluffy chair to see what the pages of this story held.

The little kitten jumped into her lap. He turned his head to the side and looked at the book with Anne Marie.

The book told the story of a brave kitten that went on a long trip with his family. Anne Marie started to read the story aloud to her kitten. The pictures in the book showed the kitten riding in the car while sitting on the lap

of a little girl. The kitten in the story looked very happy.

Anne Marie's kitten sat in her lap and purred. She stopped reading, petted his head, then scratched behind his soft ears. The kitten swatted the page.

Anne Marie picked him up so that she could see his face.

"Would you like for me to read more?" she asked.

"Meow!" said the little tiger kitten.

Anne Marie smiled. She knew just what to name her little pet.

"Your name is Books!" she said as she gave her kitten a hug.

"Meow!" Books said as he swatted another book, asking Anne Marie to read a bit more. Smiling, she opened the next book and began the story.

The End

Anne Marie and the Giant Mushroom

Challenge Words

giant

journal

mushroom

nature

pencils

Chapter One

Little Anne Marie loved to read.
She read books at home and in
her tree house.

She read books while Mother
shopped or cleaned. Sometimes
she would even read in the
bathtub!

One warm, sunny day, she and
Mother took a walk to the park
to explore the trails around it.
Anne Marie always carried her

backpack when they went to
the park so that she could have
everything she would need for an
outdoor adventure.

Her backpack held her book about the outdoors, her nature journal, and her new colored pencils, as well as bags to hold all her finds.

The park was not far from Anne Marie's house. As a game, Anne Marie and Mother counted all of the mailboxes on the way to the park.

When they got to the park, they had counted eight blue mailboxes, four red mailboxes, three yellow mailboxes, and two purple mailboxes. Anne Marie liked the purple ones the best.

Chapter Two

At the park they passed
the playground and walked
along the trails that went off
through the woods. The sun
shone and made shadows on
the ground from the big trees
over their heads.

Anne Marie could smell the forest. Dirt, grass, and trees all had a smell that made her feel happy.

Anne Marie found a patch of flowers and sat down near them to draw them in her journal. Mother smiled and sat next to her with a book to help find out what kind of flower Anne Marie was drawing. This was fun!

Anne Marie drew the flower then added a little black bug that she saw on one of the small pink flower buds. When she finished,

Anne Marie asked Mother if they could keep following the trail a bit longer.

Chapter Three

As Anne Marie and Mother turned a corner in the trail, Anne Marie saw something that looked like a large ball near a tree stump.

"Mother! Someone lost a ball in the woods! Come look with me!" she said.

She ran to take a closer look. It was not a ball! The big white thing was growing from the ground.

Anne Marie cried, "Mother, hurry! Please come and see what I have found!"

Anne Marie and Mother stooped down to look at the big white ball.

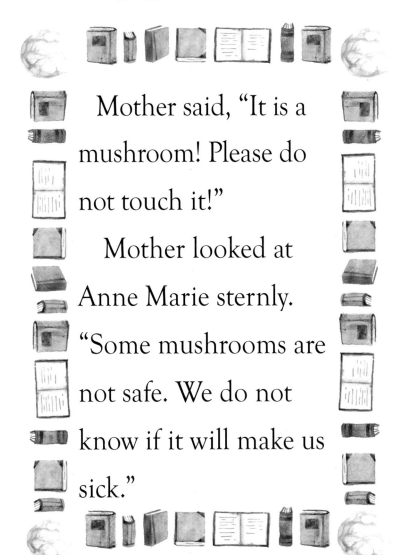

Mother said, "It is a mushroom! Please do not touch it!"

Mother looked at Anne Marie sternly. "Some mushrooms are not safe. We do not know if it will make us sick."

"But we eat mushrooms, Mother! Why would this one make me sick?" Anne Marie looked at Mother.

She did not understand
why she could not touch this
mushroom.

"You must be very careful about
mushrooms found in the wild
and never touch them unless you
ask someone who would know
for sure what they are," Mother
told her.

Chapter Four

Mother and Anne Marie
stooped down near the big
snow-white mushroom.

They looked at the top, which
was white with brown spots.
They looked at the bottom and
then the sides to see where it

was growing from and how.

After they looked at the mushroom closely, they sat down on the ground near it.

Mother showed Anne Marie a chapter in her book about wild mushrooms.

It told about all the kinds of mushrooms and gave a picture for each.

Some were funny looking while

others just looked yucky.

Then, Anne Marie found the
big white mushroom in her book!

"Giant Puffball
Mushroom," she read.
"The giant puffball
mushroom grows in
meadows, fields, and
forests in late summer
and fall."

She looked up at
Mother and smiled.

"These mushrooms can grow to over 30 inches wide and look like a white soccer ball."

"Mother!" she said, jumping up and down. "Let's add this to our nature journal!"

Anne Marie pulled her new colored pencils and her journal out of her backpack. She and Mother drew the giant puffball mushroom in the book.

Chapter Five

After they drew the giant puffball mushroom, Anne Marie looked up at Mother.

"I think we should leave the mushroom for someone else to find. We had fun looking at it, and I think others will, too!"

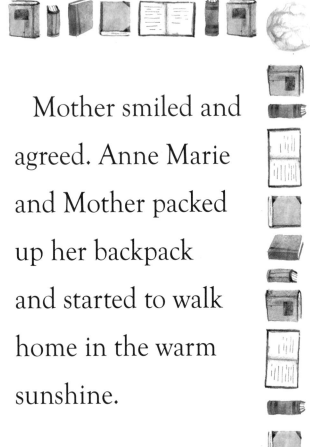

Mother smiled and agreed. Anne Marie and Mother packed up her backpack and started to walk home in the warm sunshine.

The walk home took longer than the walk to the park, as there were always so many fun items to collect. On the way home, instead of counting mailboxes, they found more little flowers, a few small rocks that shone in the sun, and they filled a bag full of acorns for Anne Marie to use for making crafts.

Chapter Six

At home Anne Marie took all
of her finds out of her backpack.
She put the little flowers in a
small teacup with a bit of water
and placed the rocks on her
window ledge to shine in the
sun. She put her acorns at her art

table and sat down to look at her
nature journal one more time.
She wanted to see the puffball
mushroom again.

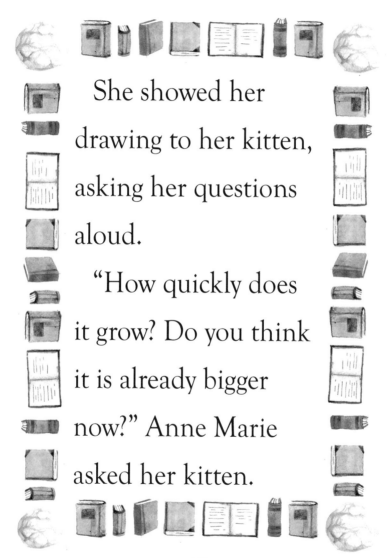

She showed her drawing to her kitten, asking her questions aloud.

"How quickly does it grow? Do you think it is already bigger now?" Anne Marie asked her kitten.

"What happens when it is done growing? Who named it a puffball mushroom?"

Anne Marie had many ideas to think about. She flipped to the page in her book that told about the mushroom and began to read.

"Anne Marie, it is dinner time!" Mother called from downstairs. Anne Marie closed her book and went to the bathroom to wash her hands for dinner.

Father was home from work when Anne Marie came to the table for dinner. Mother was putting steaming hot pasta on their plates. Anne Marie helped her father set the table by getting each of them a big glass of milk as well as a fork and napkin. She liked to help set up for dinner.

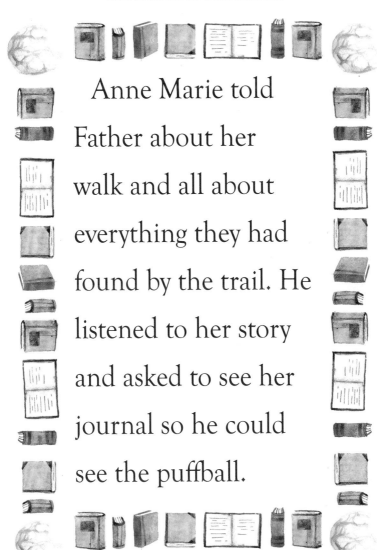

Anne Marie told Father about her walk and all about everything they had found by the trail. He listened to her story and asked to see her journal so he could see the puffball.

As they sat at the table to eat, Anne Marie looked down at her plate and giggled. Smiling, Mother looked at Anne Marie and winked her left eye. She had made pasta with chicken and mushrooms for dinner!

The End

Facts about Giant Puffball Mushrooms

Giant puffball mushrooms are *edible* (which means they are safe to eat) if they are identified correctly by an adult who knows what to look for and if they are *harvested* (picked) at the right time of their growth.

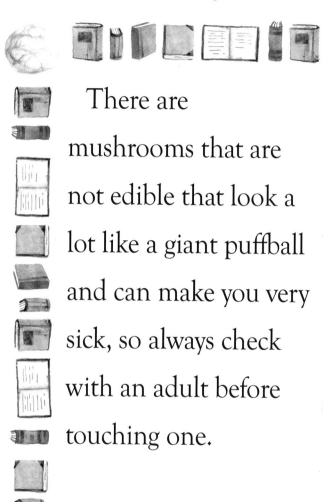

There are mushrooms that are not edible that look a lot like a giant puffball and can make you very sick, so always check with an adult before touching one.

Giant puffball mushrooms taste like tofu and are soft like a table mushroom. They can be cooked for eating or used as medicine, too. Their spores can be used to slow bleeding and were used by Native Americans to treat wounds and prevent infection.